This book is dedicated to Mrs. Johnson.

CHAIRS ON STRIKE

Jennifer Jones

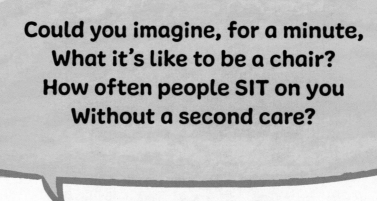

Sometimes the kids at school
Sit down hard without any care.
And boy, oh boy, it hurts us.
It simply is NOT fair.

When we're used at lunch time,
Food is smeared on us all around.
Mustard, ketchup, and some things we don't like,
But we never make a sound.

None of this is as bad for a chair
As the very worst, stinkiest part,
When a child or adult sits on us
And lets out a yucky FART!

We gathered in the classroom late at night,
And wrote some letters to discuss our needs.

For a full day during class,
The kids were forced to stand.
A couple of kids forgot and tried to sit down,
But on their bottoms they did land!

While it was fun for several hours,
The kids started to get sick of the game.
They were able to do all their schoolwork,
But it just wasn't the same.

So they took out their pencils and paper,
And they wrote us each a letter back.
Once done, they left it at their desks,
And ran to the cafeteria for a snack.

"We're sorry we treated you badly," one said.
"It's not on purpose, you see.
We didn't realize we were disrespectful.
Chair, you are so important to me."